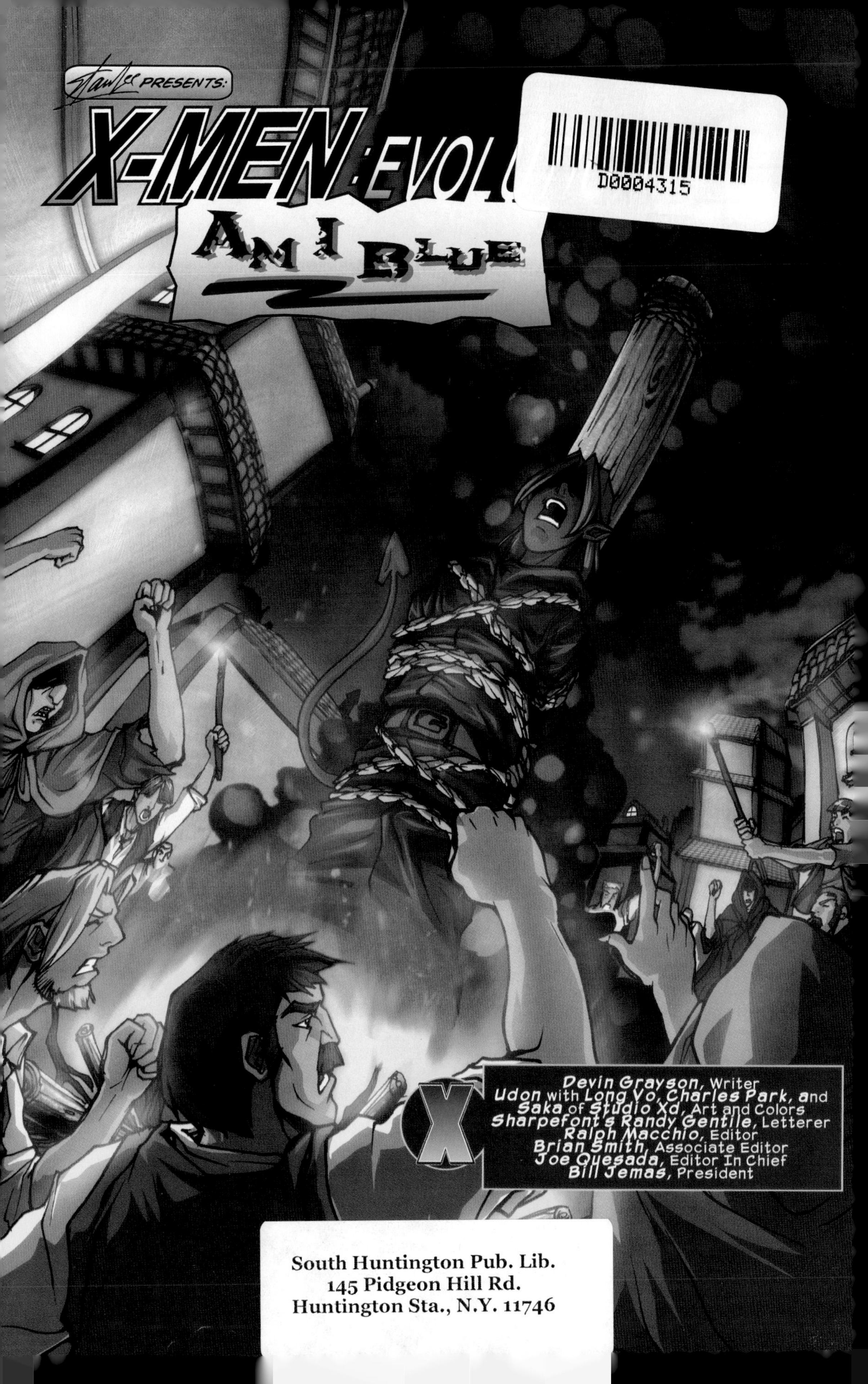
Stan Lee PRESENTS:
X-MEN: EVOLU
AM I BLUE
Devin Grayson, Writer
Udon with Long Vo, Charles Park, and Saka of Studio Xd, Art and Colors
Sharpefont's Randy Gentile, Letterer
Ralph Macchio, Editor
Brian Smith, Associate Editor
Joe Quesada, Editor In Chief
Bill Jemas, President

VISIT US AT
www.abdopublishing.com

Spotlight, a division of ABDO Publishing Company Inc., is the school and library distributor of the Marvel Entertainment books.

Library bound edition © 2006

Library of Congress Cataloging-in-Publication Data

Grayson, Devin K.
    Am I blue / Devin Grayson, writer ; Udon with Long Vo, Charles Park, and Saka, art and colors ; Randy Gentile, letterer. -- Library bound ed.
        p. cm. -- (X-Men, evolution)
    "Marvel age"--Cover.
    Revision of the May 2002 issue of X-Men.
    ISBN-13: 978-1-59961-052-8
    ISBN-10: 1-59961-052-3
    1. Graphic novels. I. Udon. II. X-Men (New York, N.Y. : 1995) III. Title. IV. Series.

PN6728.X2G73 2006
741.5'9--dc22

                                            2006043970

All Spotlight books are reinforced library binding and manufactured in the United States of America.

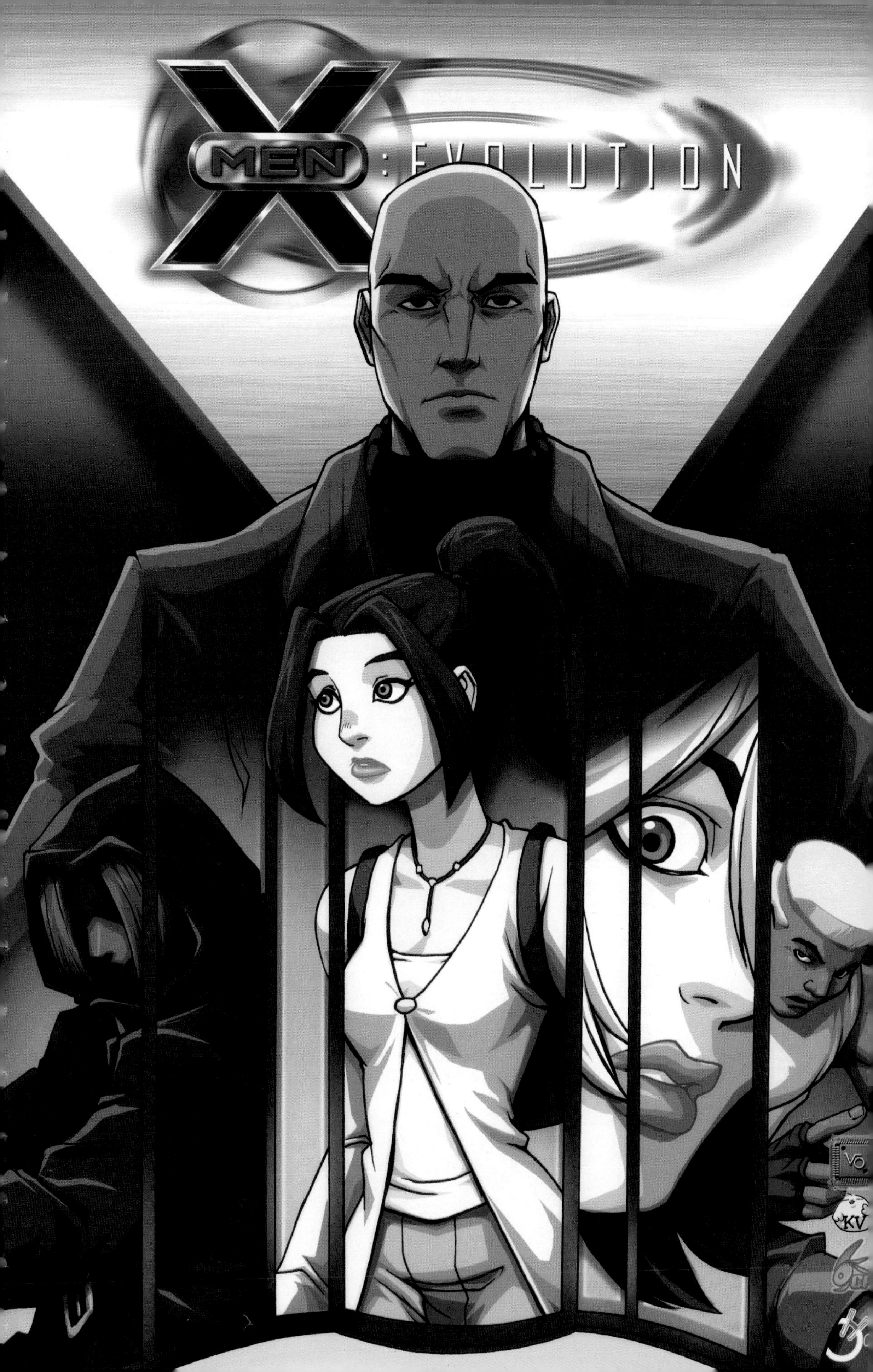
X
MEN
: EVOLUTION

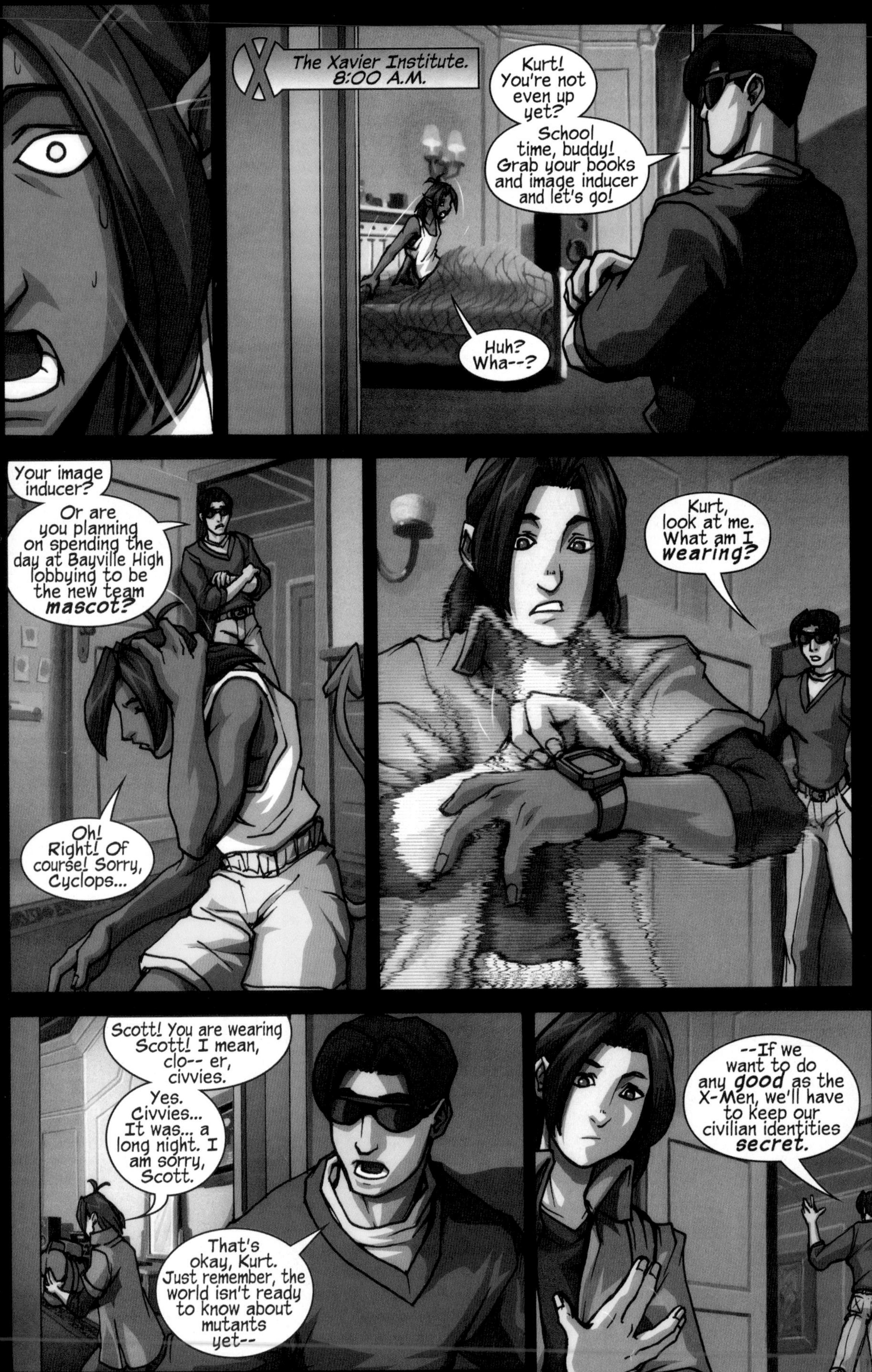

The Xavier Institute. 8:00 A.M.
Kurt! You're not even up yet?
School time, buddy! Grab your books and image inducer and let's go!
Huh? Wha--?
Your image inducer?
Or are you planning on spending the day at Bayville High lobbying to be the new team mascot?
Oh! Right! Of course! Sorry, Cyclops...
Kurt, look at me. What am I wearing?
Scott! You are wearing Scott! I mean, clo-- er, civvies.
Yes. Civvies... It was... a long night. I am sorry, Scott.
That's okay, Kurt. Just remember, the world isn't ready to know about mutants yet--
--If we want to do any good as the X-Men, we'll have to keep our civilian identities secret.

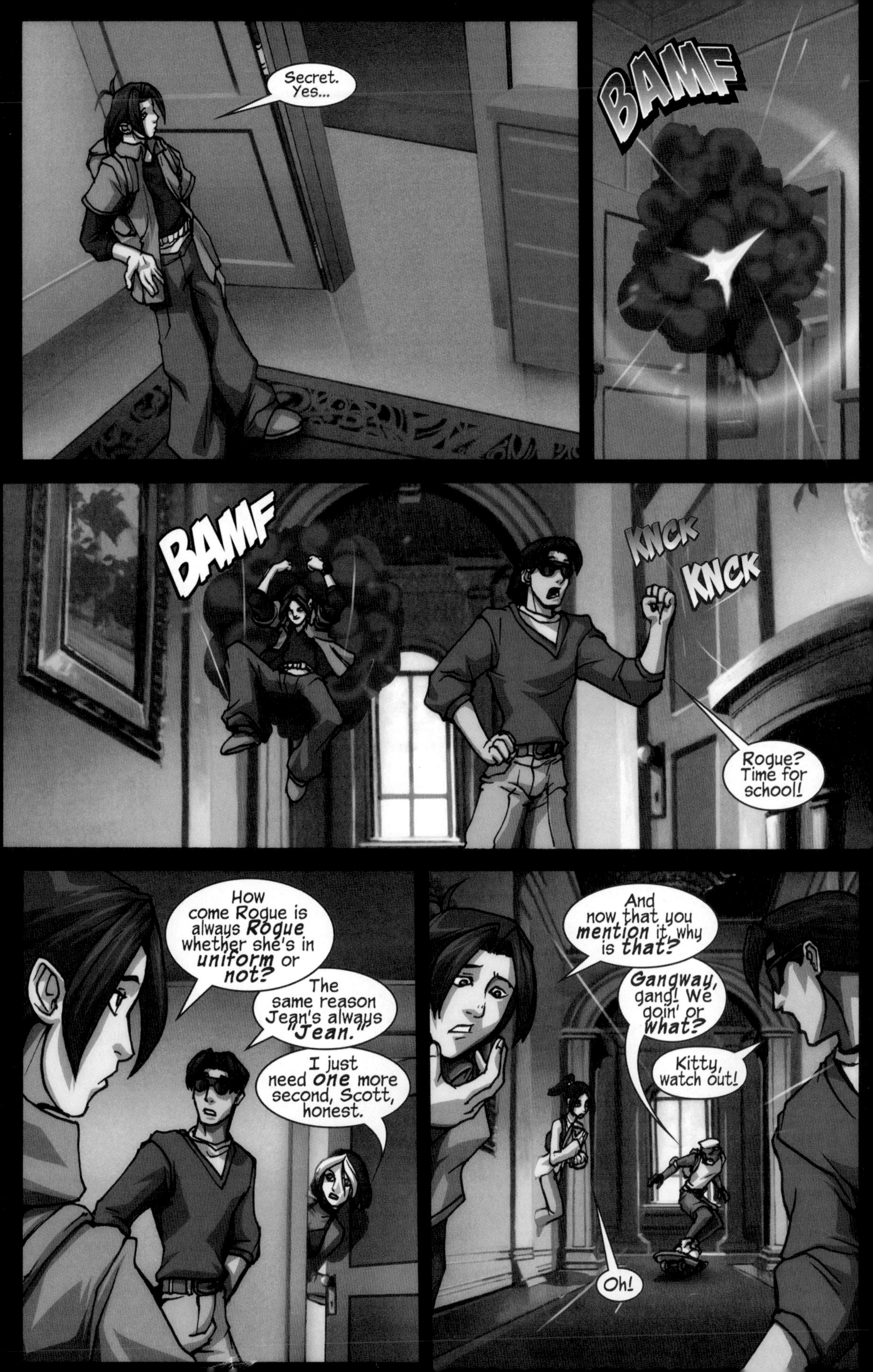
Secret. Yes...
BAMF
BAMF
KNCK KNCK
Rogue? Time for school!
How come Rogue is always Rogue whether she's in uniform or not?
The same reason Jean's always "Jean."
I just need one more second, Scott, honest.
And now that you mention it, why is that?
Gangway, gang! We goin' or what?
Kitty, watch out!
Oh!

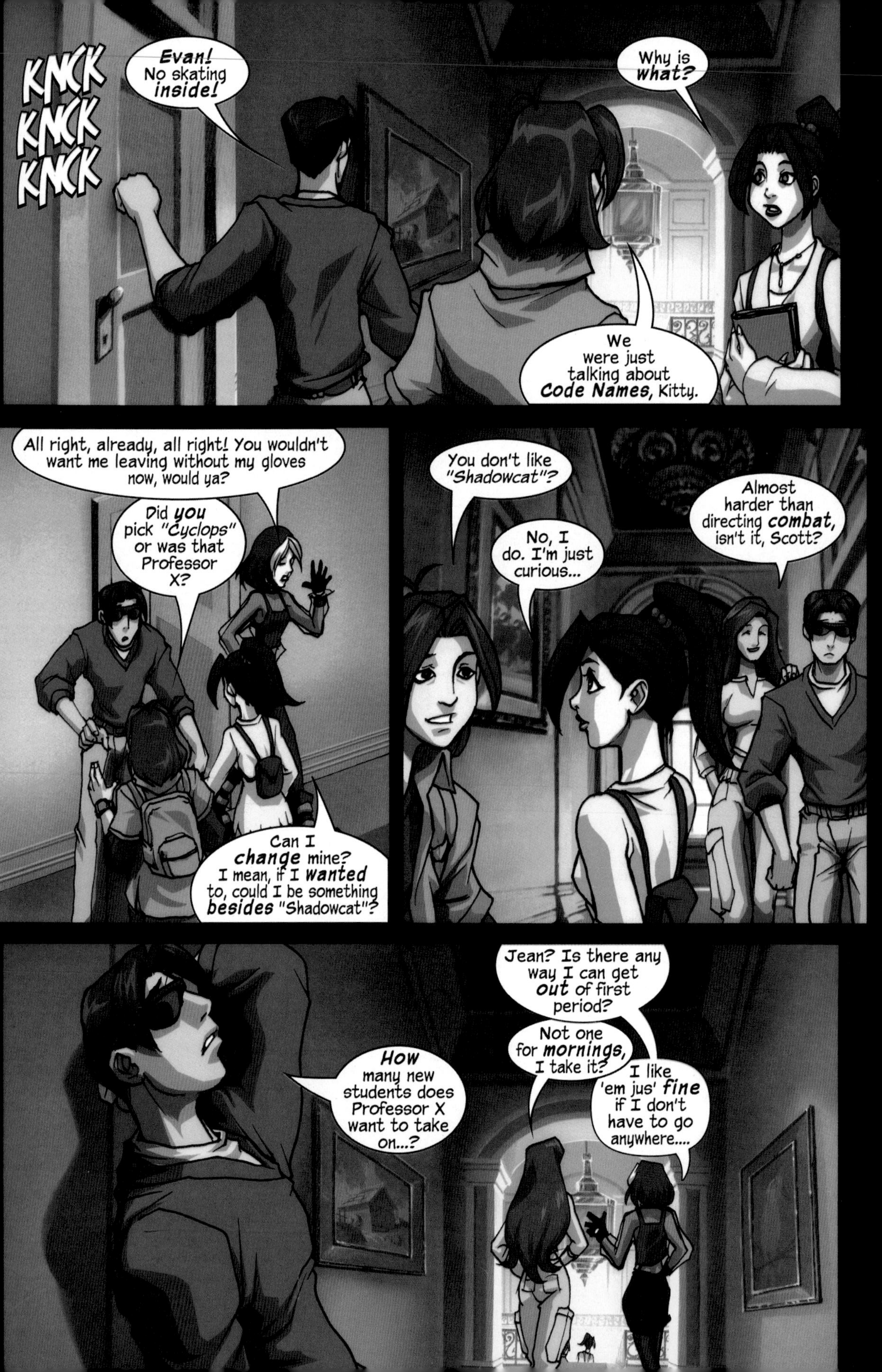
KNCK KNCK KNCK
Evan! No skating inside!
Why is what?
We were just talking about Code Names, Kitty.
All right, already, all right! You wouldn't want me leaving without my gloves now, would ya?
Did you pick "Cyclops" or was that Professor X?
Can I change mine? I mean, if I wanted to, could I be something besides "Shadowcat"?
You don't like "Shadowcat"?
No, I do. I'm just curious...
Almost harder than directing combat, isn't it, Scott?
How many new students does Professor X want to take on...?
Jean? Is there any way I can get out of first period?
Not one for mornings, I take it?
I like 'em jus' fine if I don't have to go anywhere....

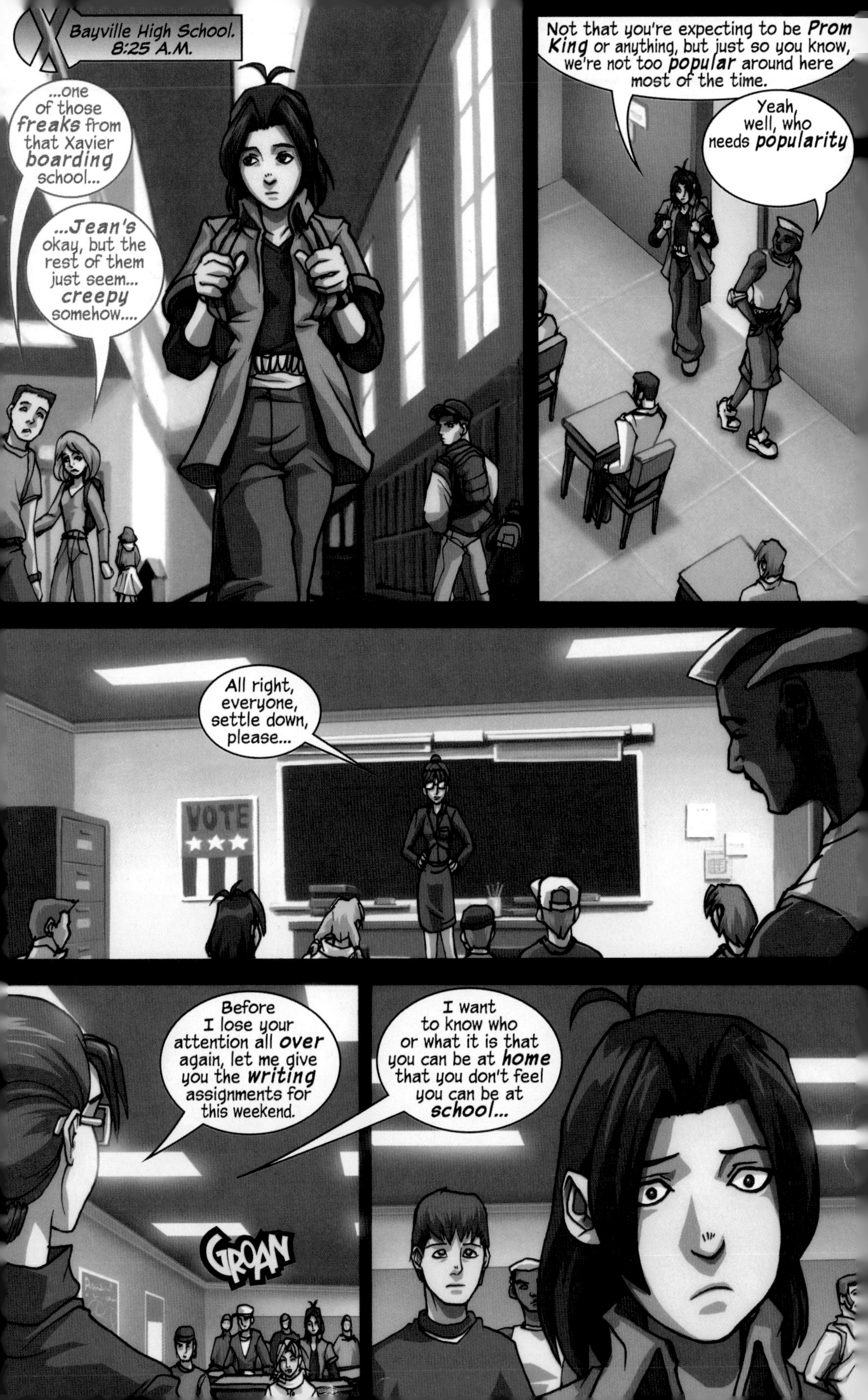
Bayville High School. 8:25 A.M.
...one of those freaks from that Xavier boarding school...
...Jean's okay, but the rest of them just seem... creepy somehow....
Not that you're expecting to be Prom King or anything, but just so you know, we're not too popular around here most of the time.
Yeah, well, who needs popularity
All right, everyone, settle down, please...
VOTE
Before I lose your attention all over again, let me give you the writing assignments for this weekend.
GROAN
I want to know who or what it is that you can be at home that you don't feel you can be at school...

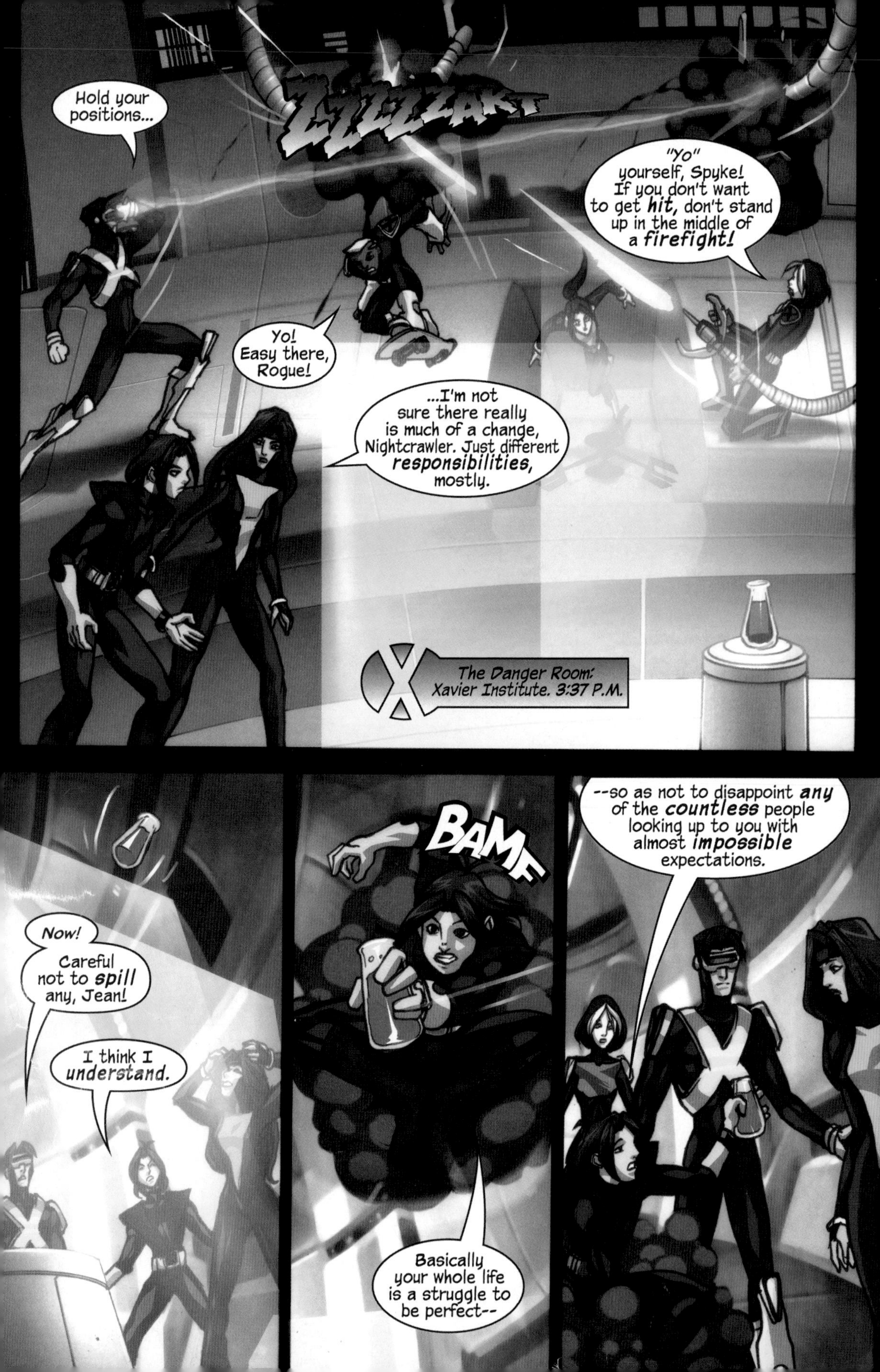
Hold your positions...
ZZZZZAKT
"Yo" yourself, Spyke! If you don't want to get hit, don't stand up in the middle of a firefight!
Yo! Easy there, Rogue!
...I'm not sure there really is much of a change, Nightcrawler. Just different responsibilities, mostly.
The Danger Room: Xavier Institute. 3:37 P.M.
Now!
Careful not to spill any, Jean!
I think I understand.
BAMF
Basically your whole life is a struggle to be perfect--
--so as not to disappoint any of the countless people looking up to you with almost impossible expectations.

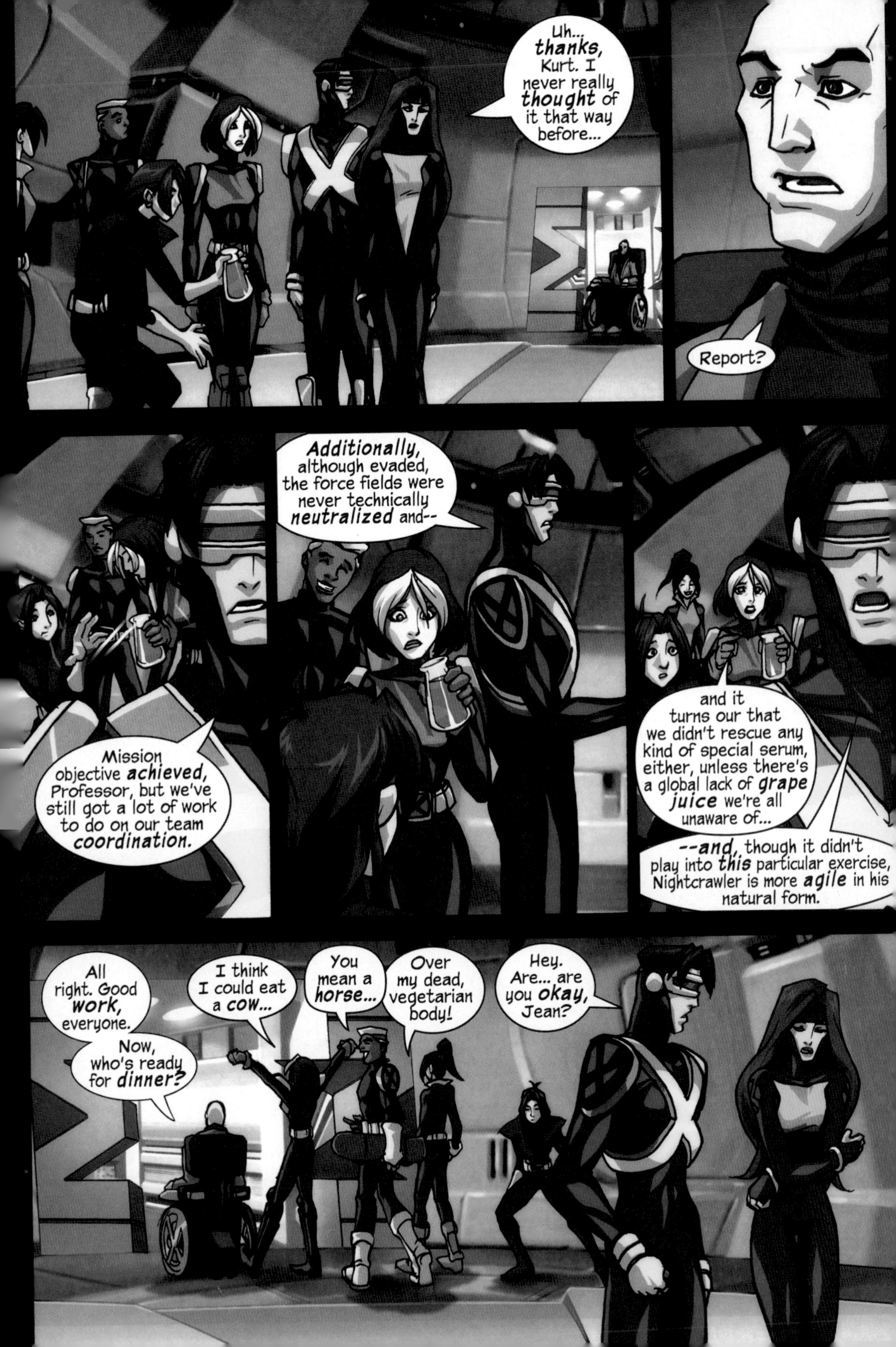
Uh... thanks, Kurt. I never really thought of it that way before...
Report?
Mission objective achieved, Professor, but we've still got a lot of work to do on our team coordination.
Additionally, although evaded, the force fields were never technically neutralized and--
and it turns our that we didn't rescue any kind of special serum, either, unless there's a global lack of grape juice we're all unaware of...
--and, though it didn't play into this particular exercise, Nightcrawler is more agile in his natural form.
All right. Good work, everyone.
Now, who's ready for dinner?
I think I could eat a cow...
You mean a horse...
Over my dead, vegetarian body!
Hey. Are... are you okay, Jean?

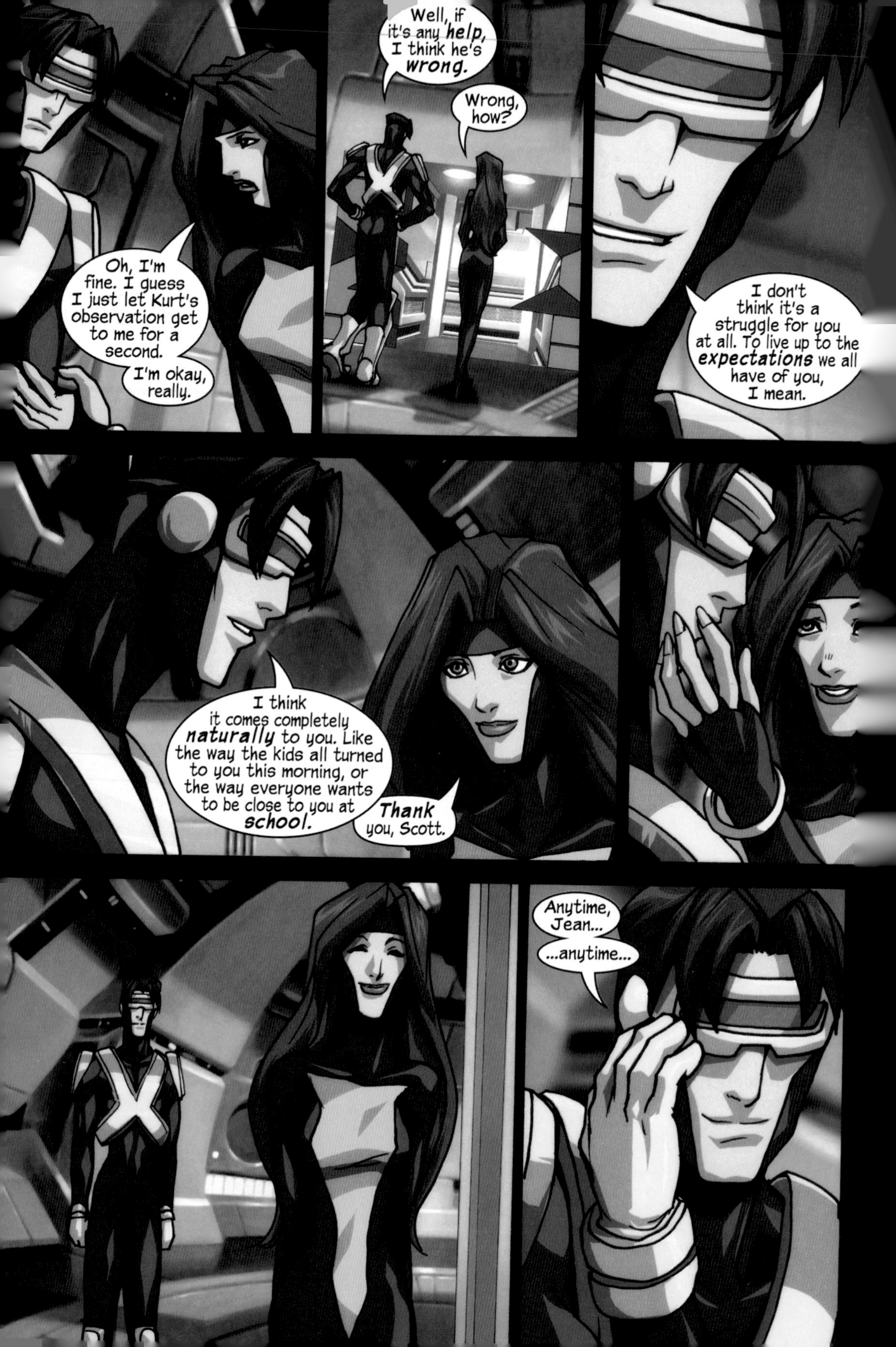
Oh, I'm fine. I guess I just let Kurt's observation get to me for a second.
I'm okay, really.
Well, if it's any help, I think he's wrong.
Wrong, how?
I don't think it's a struggle for you at all. To live up to the expectations we all have of you, I mean.
I think it comes completely naturally to you. Like the way the kids all turned to you this morning, or the way everyone wants to be close to you at school.
Thank you, Scott.
Anytime, Jean...
...anytime...

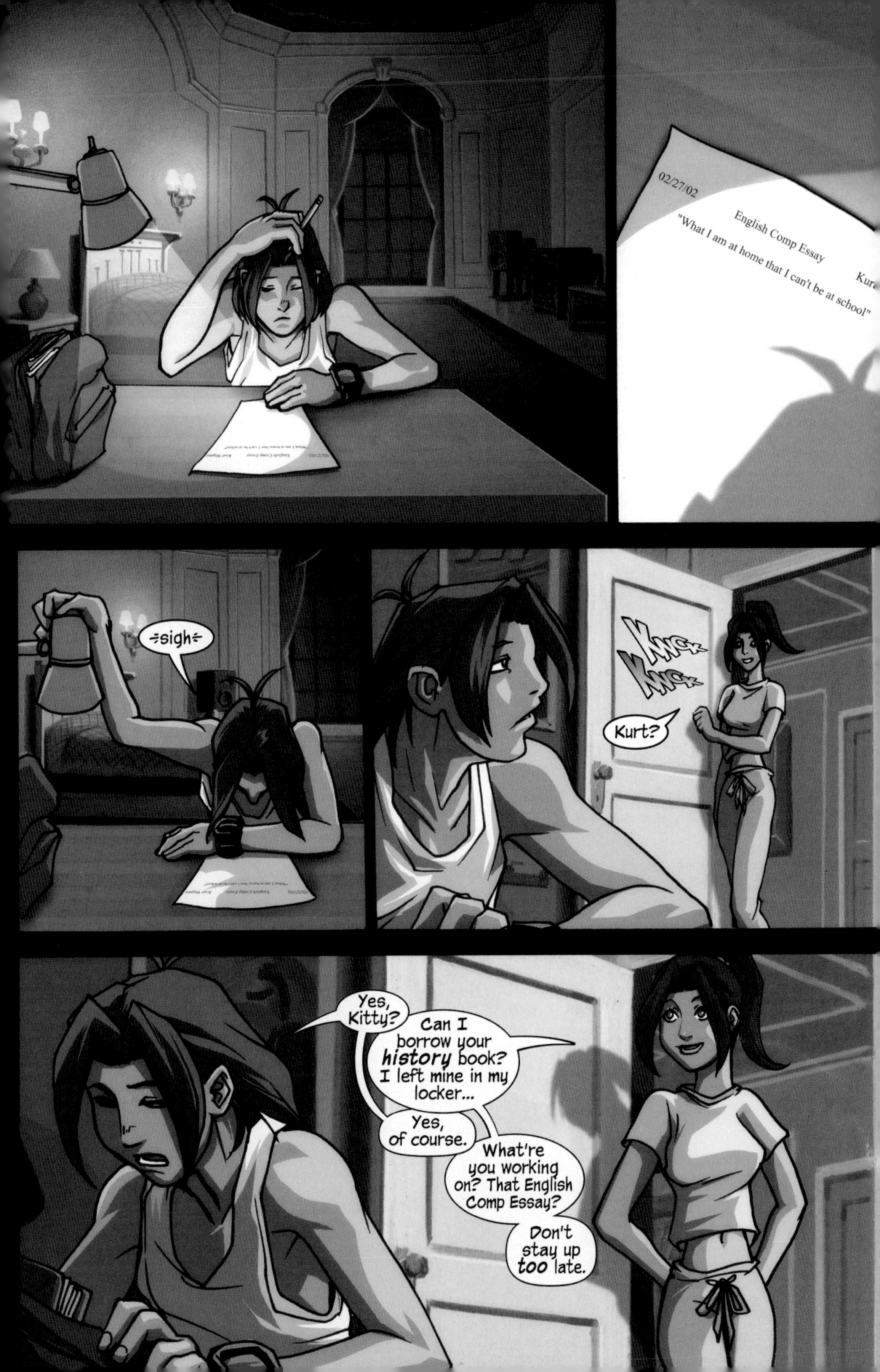
02/27/02
English Comp Essay
Kur
"What I am at home that I can't be at school"
=sigh=
KNOCK KNOCK
Kurt?
Yes, Kitty?
Can I borrow your history book? I left mine in my locker...
Yes, of course.
What're you working on? That English Comp Essay?
Don't stay up too late.

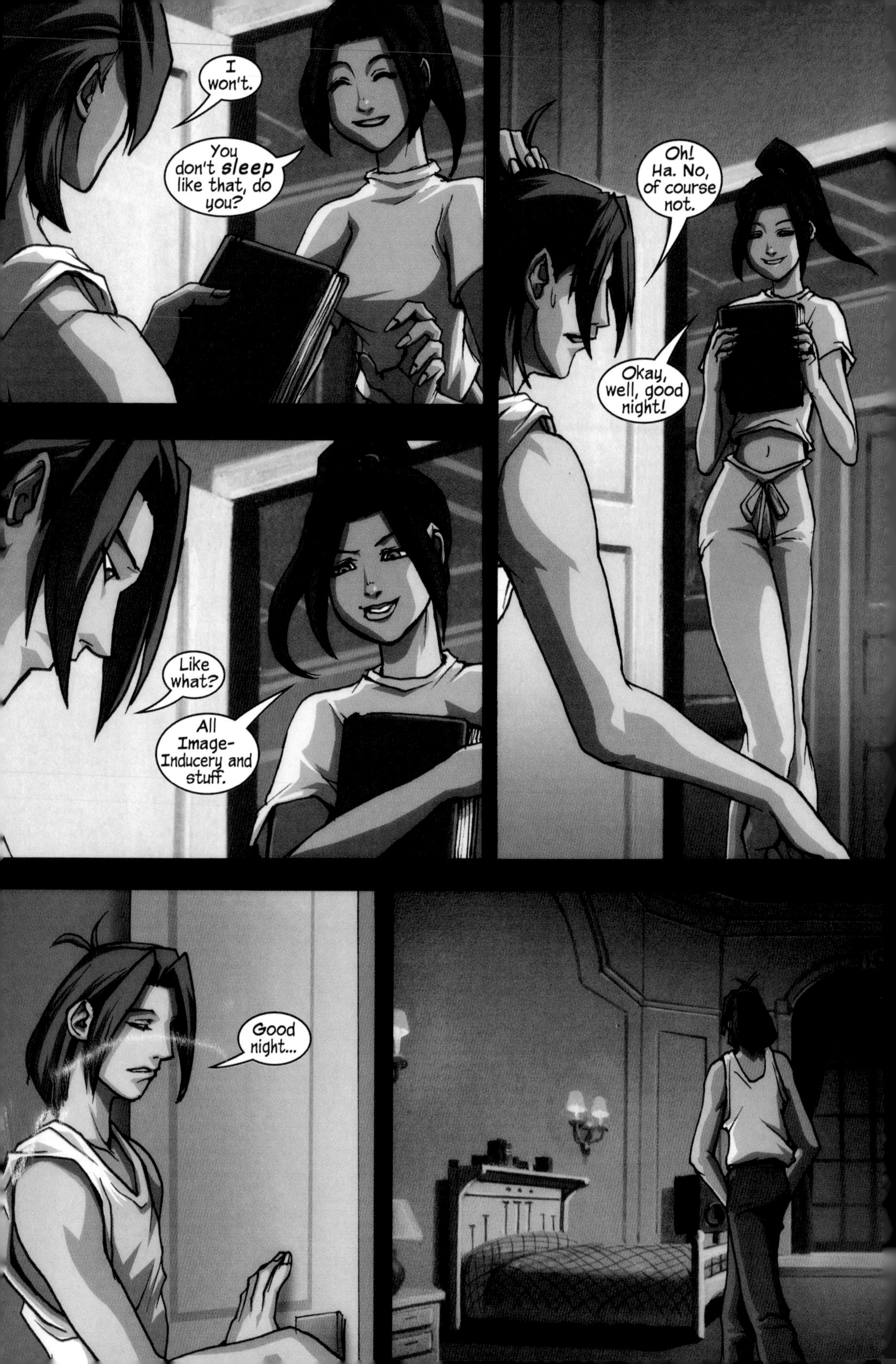
I won't.
You don't sleep like that, do you?
Oh! Ha. No, of course not.
Okay, well, good night!
Like what?
All Image-Inducery and stuff.
Good night...

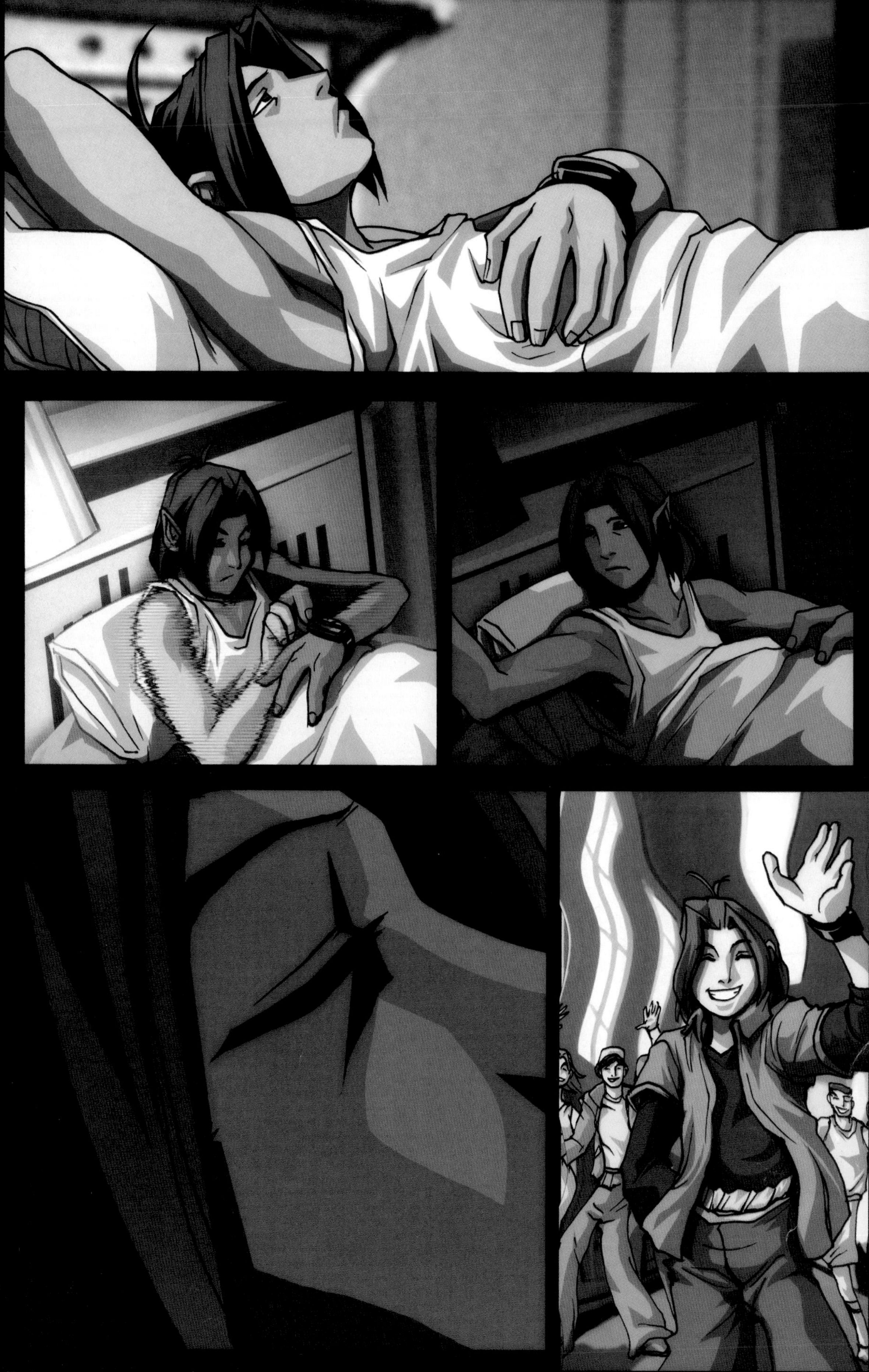

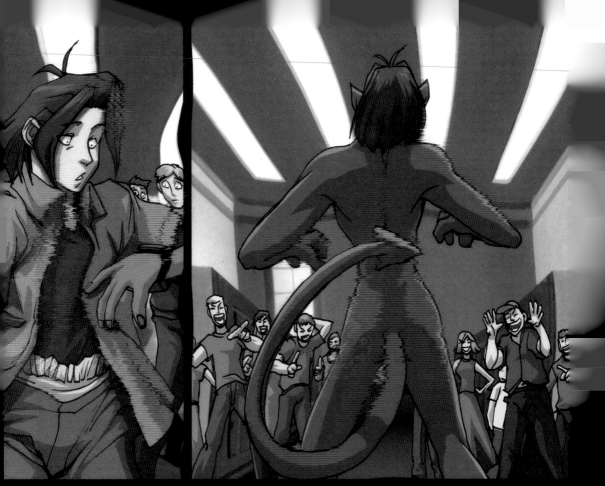

Oh...!

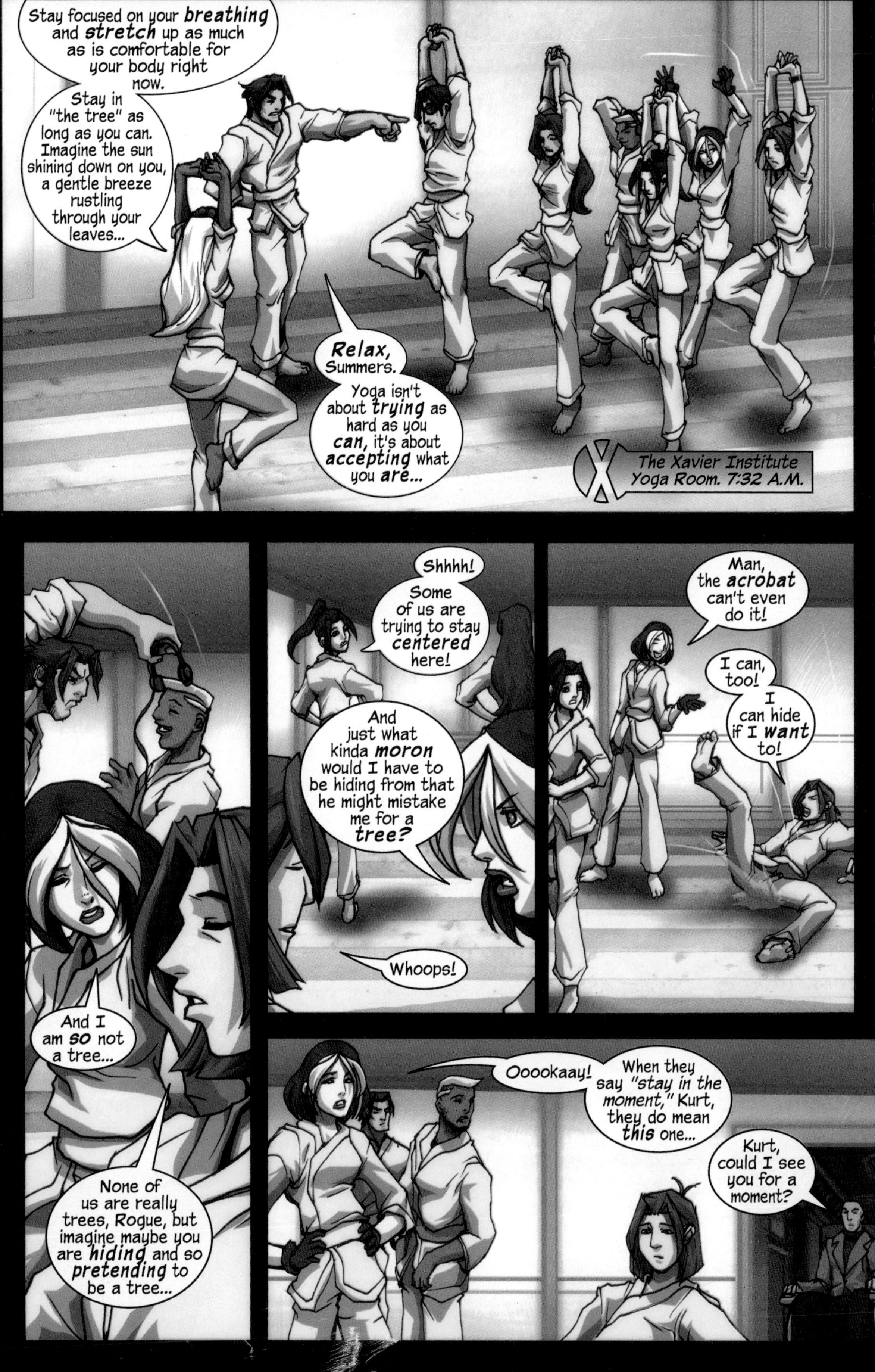
Stay focused on your breathing and stretch up as much as is comfortable for your body right now.
Stay in "the tree" as long as you can. Imagine the sun shining down on you, a gentle breeze rustling through your leaves...
Relax, Summers.
Yoga isn't about trying as hard as you can, it's about accepting what you are...
The Xavier Institute Yoga Room. 7:32 A.M.
And I am so not a tree...
None of us are really trees, Rogue, but imagine maybe you are hiding and so pretending to be a tree...
Shhhh!
Some of us are trying to stay centered here!
And just what kinda moron would I have to be hiding from that he might mistake me for a tree?
Whoops!
Man, the acrobat can't even do it!
I can, too!
I can hide if I want to!
Ooookaay!
When they say "stay in the moment," Kurt, they do mean this one...
Kurt, could I see you for a moment?

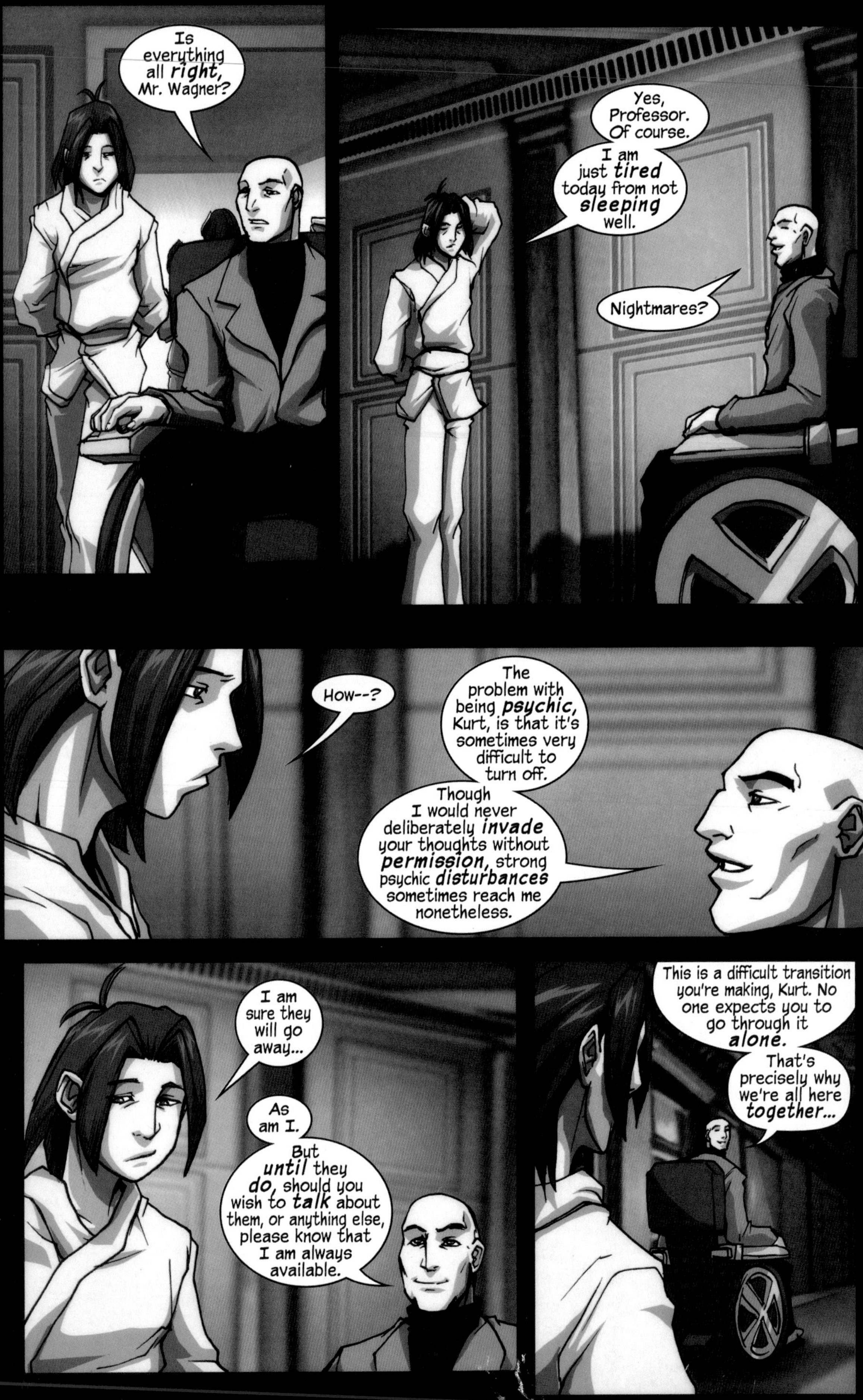

Is everything all right, Mr. Wagner?
Yes, Professor. Of course.
I am just tired today from not sleeping well.
Nightmares?
How--?
The problem with being psychic, Kurt, is that it's sometimes very difficult to turn off.
Though I would never deliberately invade your thoughts without permission, strong psychic disturbances sometimes reach me nonetheless.
I am sure they will go away...
As am I.
But until they do, should you wish to talk about them, or anything else, please know that I am always available.
This is a difficult transition you're making, Kurt. No one expects you to go through it alone.
That's precisely why we're all here together...

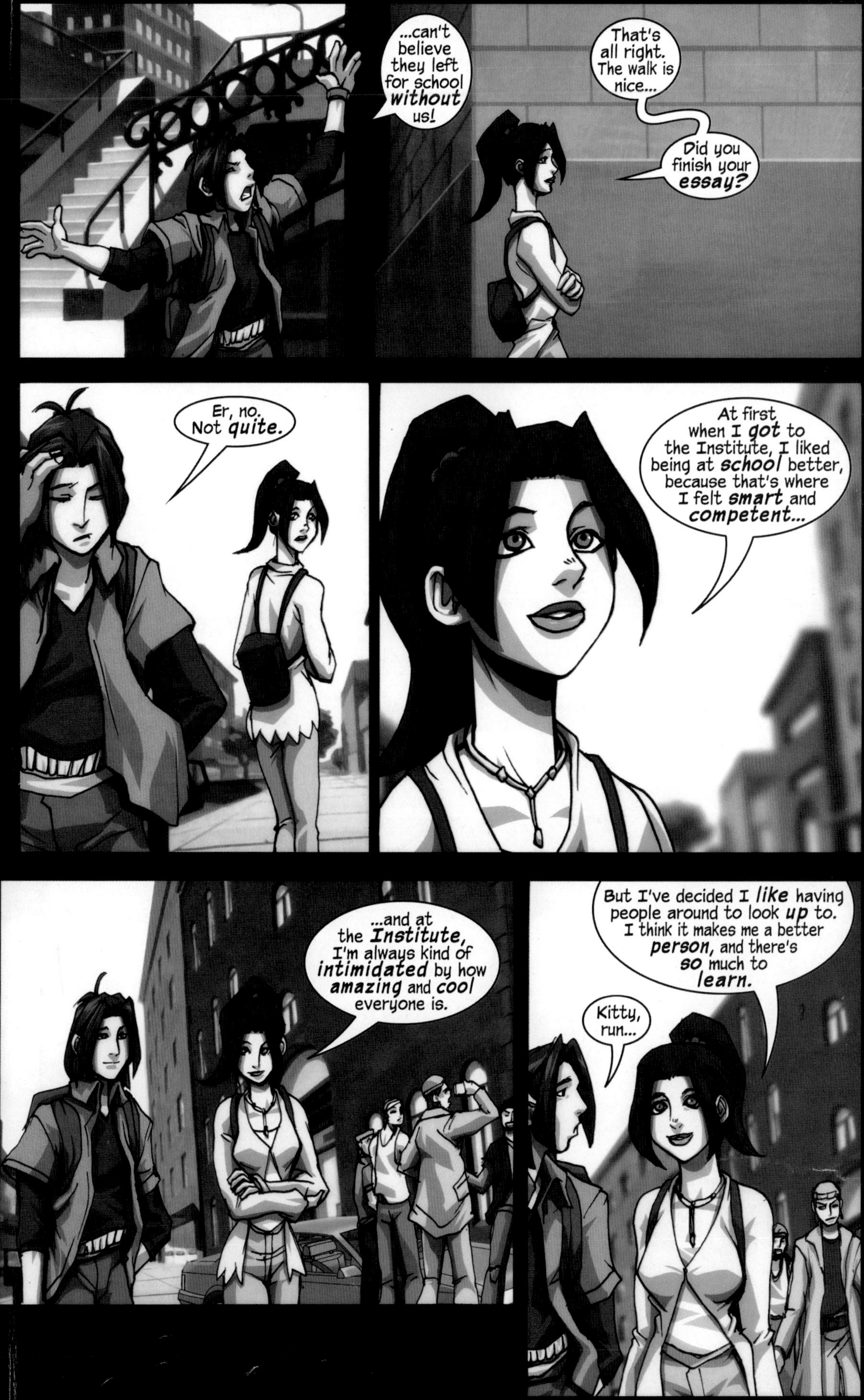
...can't believe they left for school without us!
That's all right. The walk is nice...
Did you finish your essay?
Er, no. Not quite.
At first when I got to the Institute, I liked being at school better, because that's where I felt smart and competent...
...and at the Institute, I'm always kind of intimidated by how amazing and cool everyone is.
But I've decided I like having people around to look up to. I think it makes me a better person, and there's so much to learn.
Kitty, run...

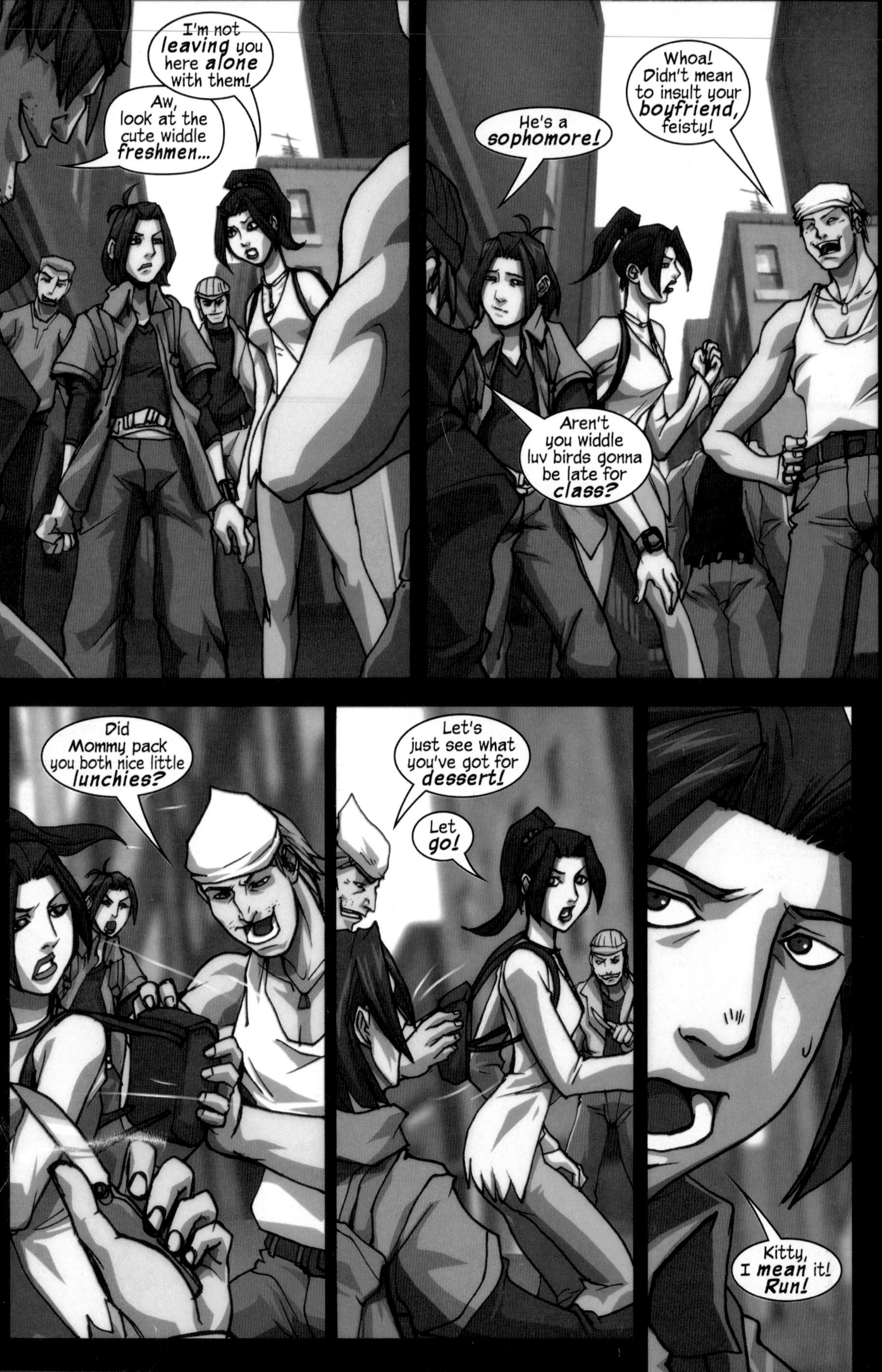
I'm not leaving you here alone with them!
Aw, look at the cute widdle freshmen...
He's a sophomore!
Whoa! Didn't mean to insult your boyfriend, feisty!
Aren't you widdle luv birds gonna be late for class?
Did Mommy pack you both nice little lunchies?
Let's just see what you've got for dessert!
Let go!
Kitty, I mean it! Run!

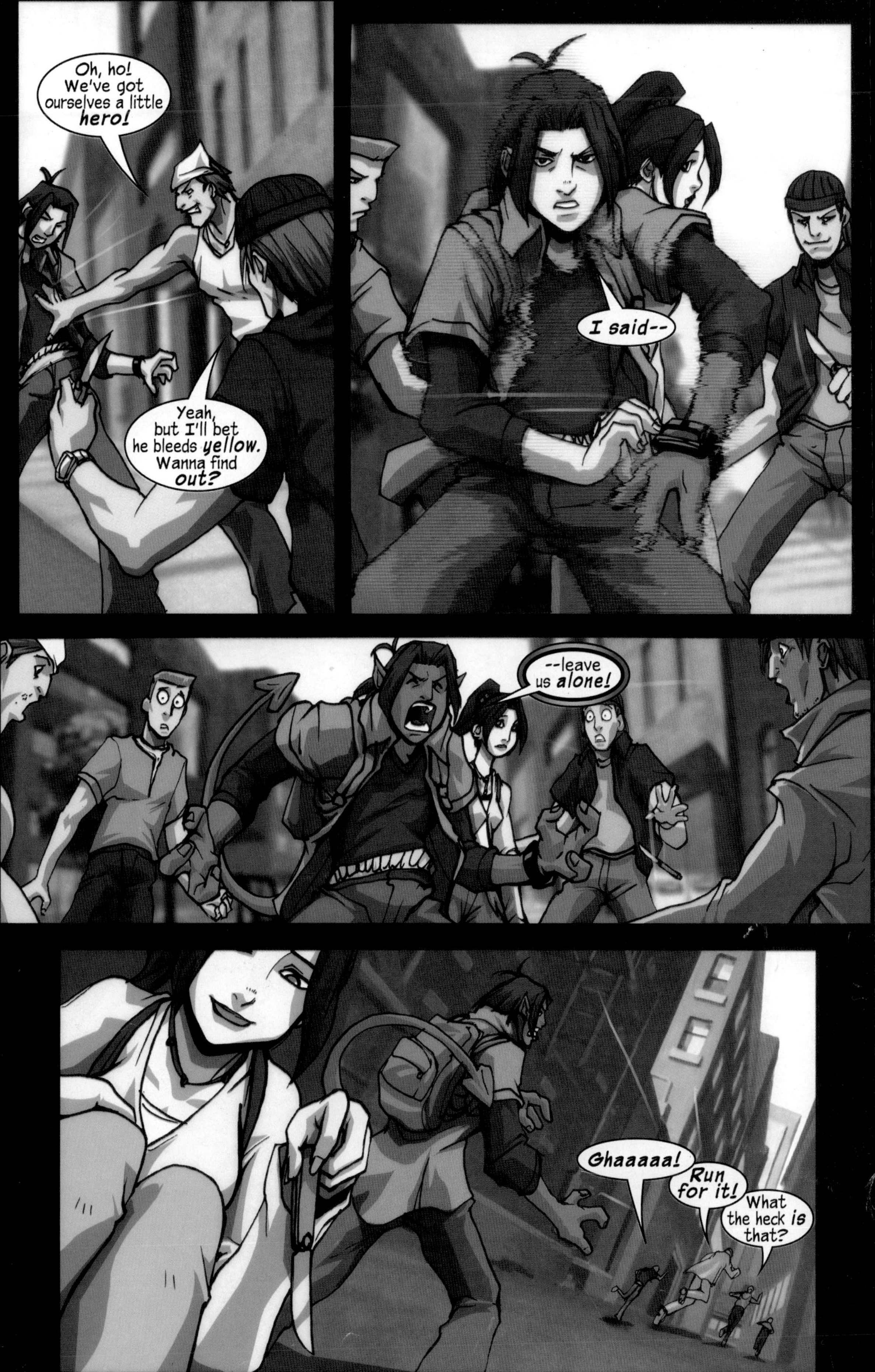
Oh, ho! We've got ourselves a little hero!
Yeah, but I'll bet he bleeds yellow. Wanna find out?
I said--
--leave us alone!
Ghaaaaa!
Run for it!
What the heck is that?

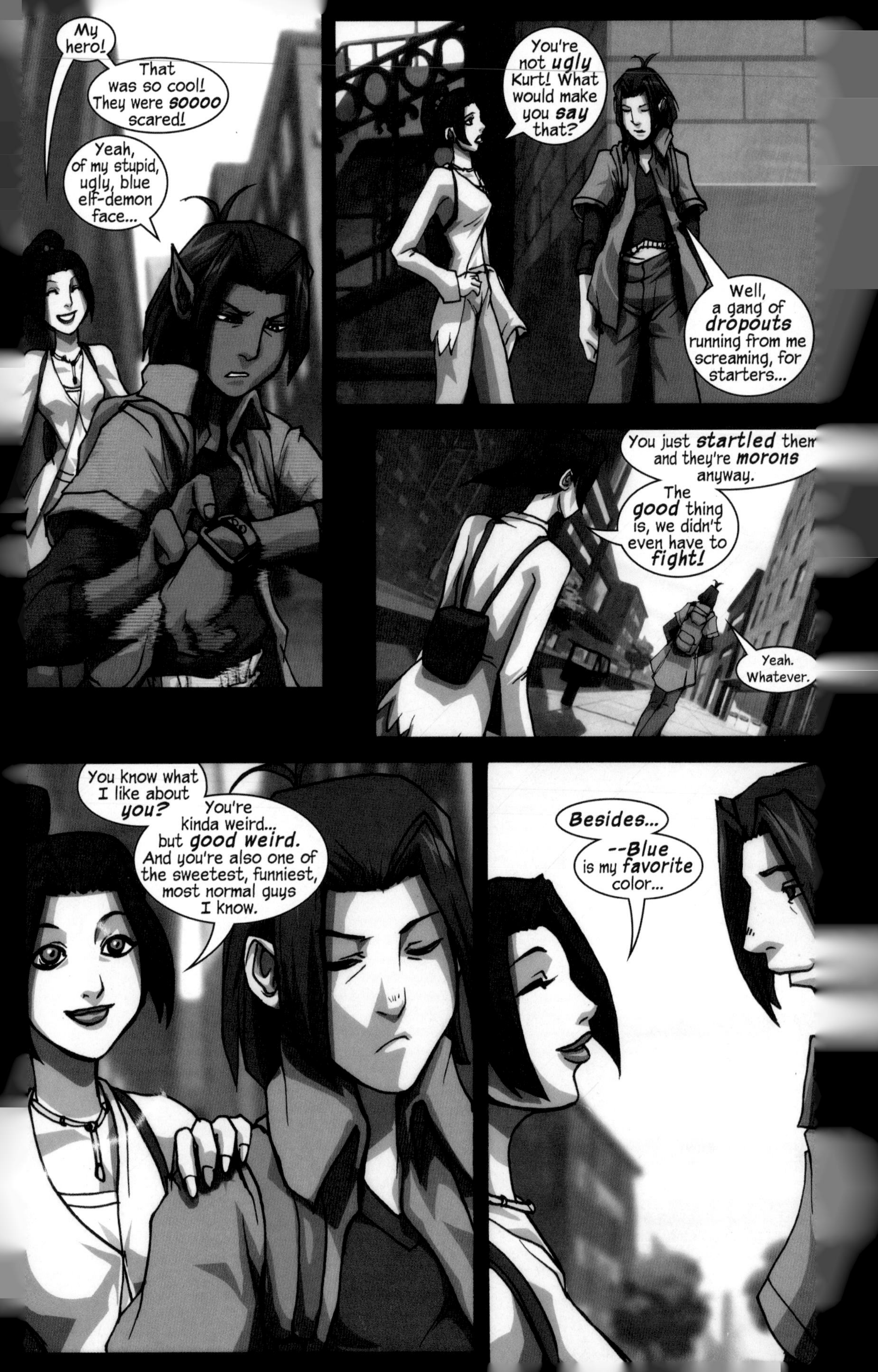
My hero!
That was so cool! They were SOOOO scared!
Yeah, of my stupid, ugly, blue elf-demon face...
You're not ugly Kurt! What would make you say that?
Well, a gang of dropouts running from me screaming, for starters...
You just startled them and they're morons anyway.
The good thing is, we didn't even have to fight!
Yeah. Whatever.
You know what I like about you?
You're kinda weird... but good weird. And you're also one of the sweetest, funniest, most normal guys I know.
Besides...
--Blue is my favorite color...

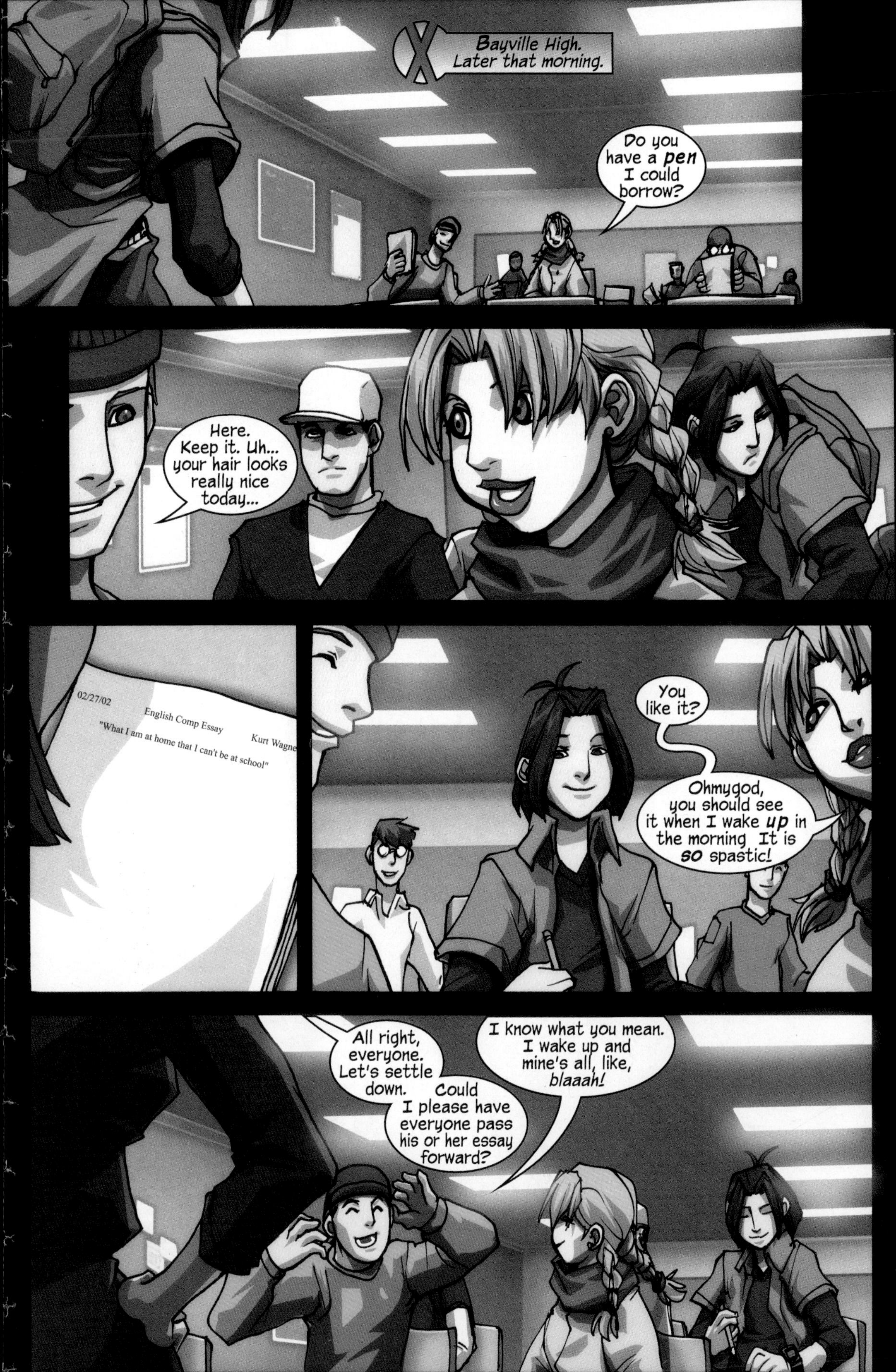
Bayville High. Later that morning.
Do you have a pen I could borrow?
Here. Keep it. Uh... your hair looks really nice today...
02/27/02
English Comp Essay
Kurt Wagne
"What I am at home that I can't be at school"
You like it?
Ohmygod, you should see it when I wake up in the morning It is SO spastic!
All right, everyone. Let's settle down.
I know what you mean. I wake up and mine's all, like, blaaah!
Could I please have everyone pass his or her essay forward?

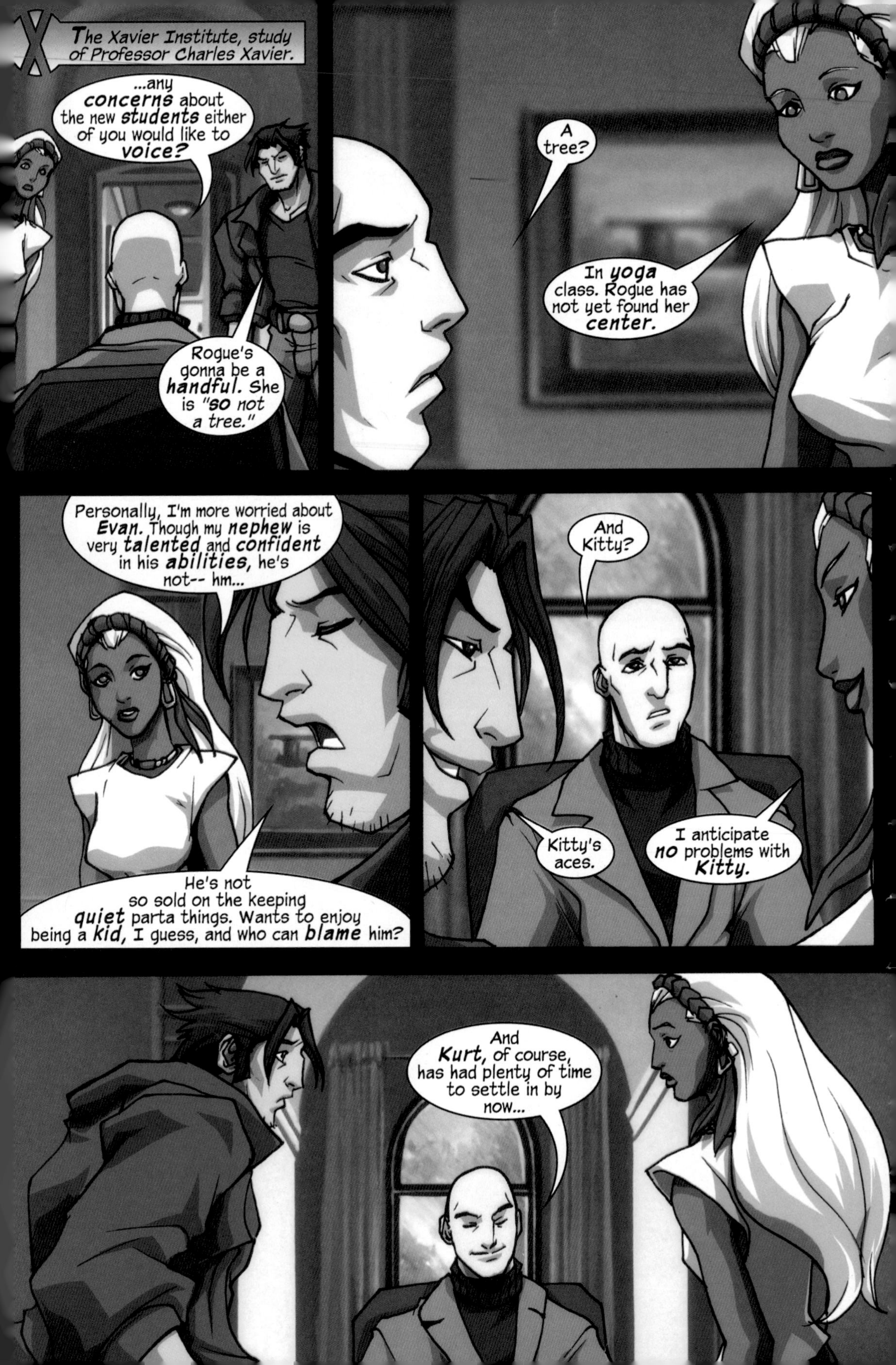
The Xavier Institute, study of Professor Charles Xavier.
...any concerns about the new students either of you would like to voice?
Rogue's gonna be a handful. She is "so not a tree."
A tree?
In yoga class. Rogue has not yet found her center.
Personally, I'm more worried about Evan. Though my nephew is very talented and confident in his abilities, he's not-- hm...
He's not so sold on the keeping quiet parta things. Wants to enjoy being a kid, I guess, and who can blame him?
And Kitty?
Kitty's aces.
I anticipate no problems with Kitty.
And Kurt, of course, has had plenty of time to settle in by now...

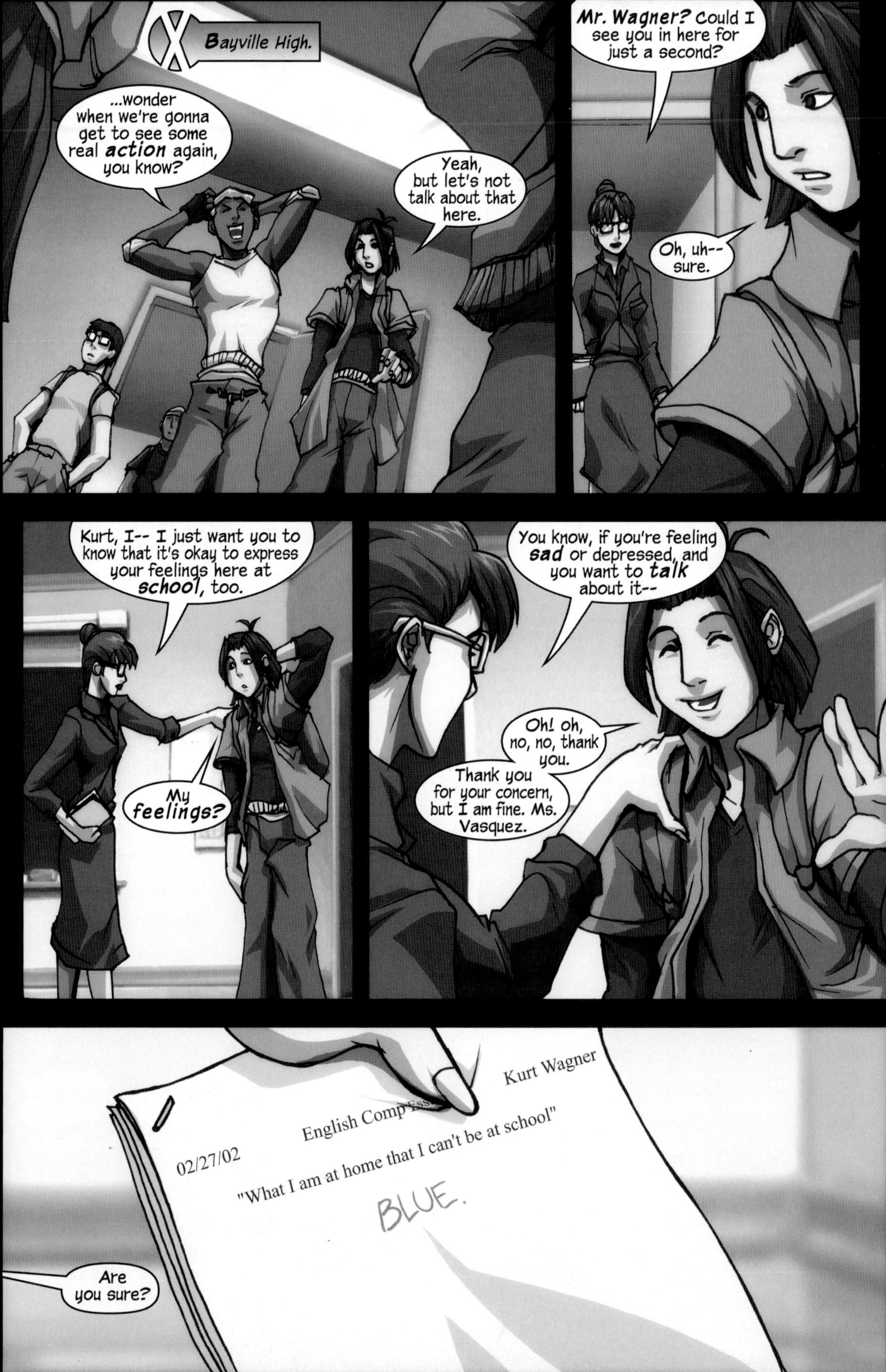
Bayville High.
...wonder when we're gonna get to see some real action again, you know?
Yeah, but let's not talk about that here.
Mr. Wagner? Could I see you in here for just a second?
Oh, uh-- sure.
Kurt, I-- I just want you to know that it's okay to express your feelings here at school, too.
My feelings?
You know, if you're feeling sad or depressed, and you want to talk about it--
Oh! oh, no, no, thank you.
Thank you for your concern, but I am fine. Ms. Vasquez.
Kurt Wagner
English Comp Ess
02/27/02
"What I am at home that I can't be at school"
BLUE.
Are you sure?

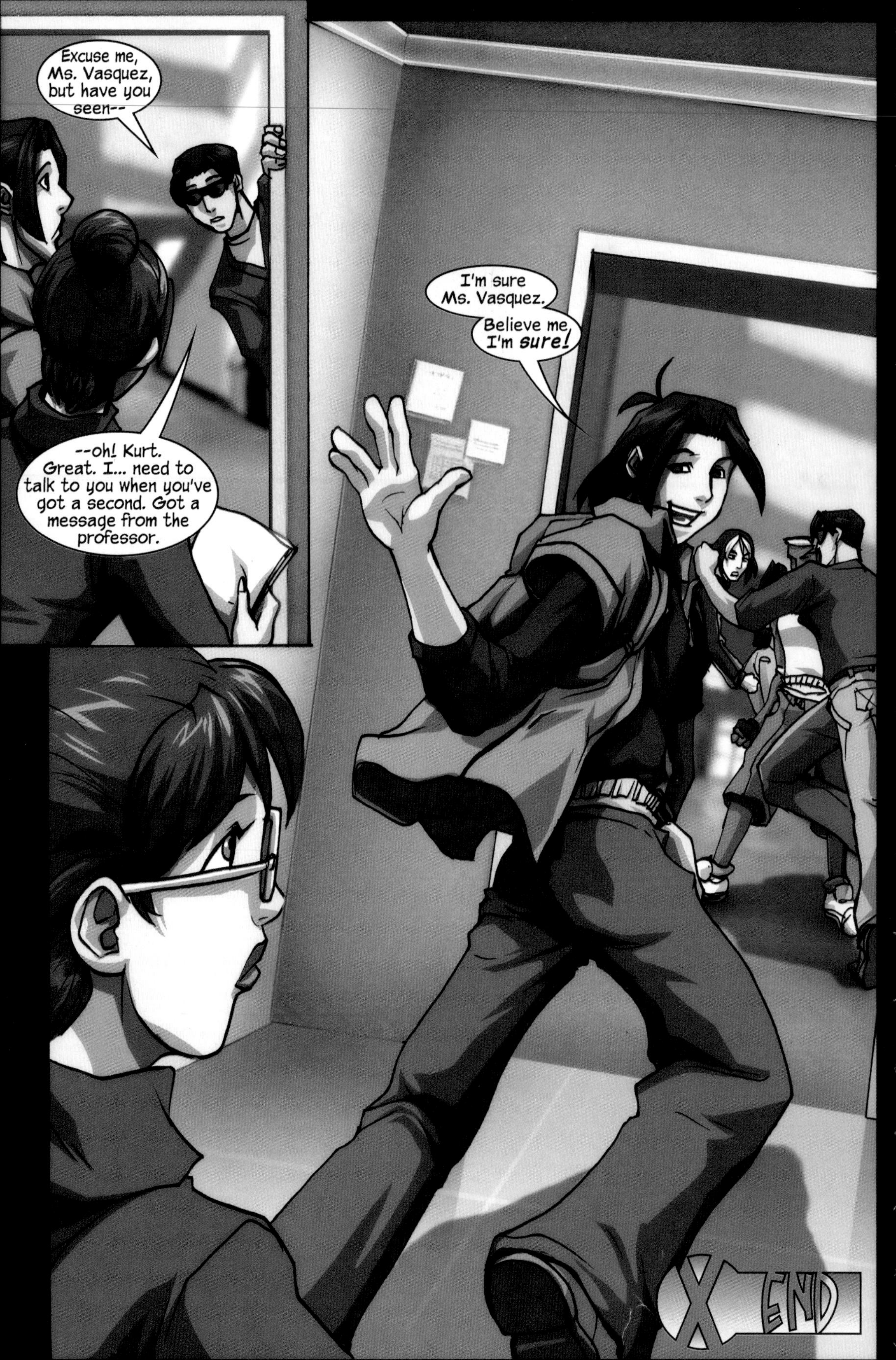
Excuse me, Ms. Vasquez, but have you seen--
--oh! Kurt. Great. I... need to talk to you when you've got a second. Got a message from the professor.
I'm sure Ms. Vasquez.
Believe me, I'm *sure!*
END